Remmy
and the Brain Train

TRAVELING THROUGH
THE LAND OF GOOD SLEEP

by Dr. James B. Maas

Illustrations by Guy Danella • Song by Suzanne Scheniman

This book is dedicated to Nancy, Daniel and Justin Maas, and was made possible through the generosity of Enid and Jerry Alpern. I am deeply indebted to Don Hoffman and Charlie Eitel for their enthusiastic efforts in helping me spread the gospel of good sleep as a necessity for health and performance, and to the Simmons Company for their dedication to better sleep through science.

Special thanks to Alexis Kahn, Sarah Cupp, Megan Wherry, Heidi and Maggie Seitz, Cindy Durbin, Janet Robinson, Rena Wax, Caryn and Roger Weiss, Mimi and William Schaffner, Carla Schaefer, Barbara Hogan, David Feldshuh, Bruce Levitt, William Dement, Mary Carskadon, David Dinges, Tom Roth, Faust Rossi, Catherine Neaher, Francesca Neaher, Rosemary Niehuss, Ginger Pape, Barbara Hall, Barbara Rowan, Robin Powers, Kari and Ken Robinson, Kristen Potter, David Myers, Ross Nadeau, David Daniels, Becky Heimerman, Brandon Palmer and United Feather and Down.

Remmy and the Brain Train
Text and illustrations copyright © 2001 by James B. Maas

Book design by Richard Nadeau, Nadeau Associates, Utica, New York. Printed by Brodock Press in the United States of America.

Library of Congress Control Number: 2001118196

ISBN 0-9712140-0-X

Remmy woke up when he heard his mom say:
"Get up and get dressed, it's another school day!"
He pulled off the covers and stretched out one arm —
His sleepy old brain never heard the alarm!

He threw on some clothes—
One white sock, one blue.
No time for a comb
Or the lace on one shoe.

A SLURP
And a SLOP
Was breakfast
And then...

He ran for the bus — almost missed it, AGAIN !

At school he discovered he just couldn't add.
The kids started laughing, his math was so bad!

3

He had to spell "ZOO" — he thought that he knew it.
He tried and he tried, but he just couldn't do it!

Time to play ball —
To the playground they dashed!
They tossed it... He missed it...
He tripped and he crashed!

What could he do? Try as he might —
His body and brain weren't working quite right!

Remmy came home and he told Mom and Dad
How THIS made him grumpy and THAT made him sad.

Dad made spaghetti — always a winner —
But Remmy was tired, and slept right through dinner!

Then Mom said, "Now Remmy, I know why you're groggy...
You stay up too late, then you wake up too foggy!
TV and toys — all those fun things to do —
The reason for sleep is a mystery to you!"

That very night as he snuggled in bed
His ears heard a voice, and here's what it said:

Hello there, Remmy! My name's Doctor Zeez.
Let's talk about sleep — listen up, if you please!
When your brain feels like mush and your eyes feel like gravel
Let me explain where's the best place to travel ...

Just hop into bed
When the day turns to night.
Your Brain Train will come
When you turn out the light!

"What is the Brain Train?
And where does it go?
And what does it do?"
Remmy wanted to know.

I'll show you all that, but before we depart—
A regular bedtime is how you should start.
A trip on the train keeps your brain at its prime
And THIS train runs best when it runs right on time!

HURRY

COME TO THE STATION,
HOP ON THE TRAIN.
YOU DON'T NEED A TICKET —
JUST PACK UP YOUR BRAIN!
ROCK WITH THE RHYTHM
AND COUNT ALL THE SHEEP
CLICKETY-CLACK
TO THE LAND OF GOOD SLEEP!

The Brain Train will take things that happened today
To the Land of Good Sleep, where it puts them away...

Saving each one as a MEMORY TRACE
Carefully stashed in its own little place.

You'll make traces for letters, traces for names,
Spelling... and math... and how to play games.

With all of your traces in all the right places...
You won't forget homework or lunches or laces!

You'll never forget things that nice people do
Or that wombat and wildebeest down at the zoo.
You'll never forget P comes right before Q
Or the answer to NINE minus SEVEN is TWO!

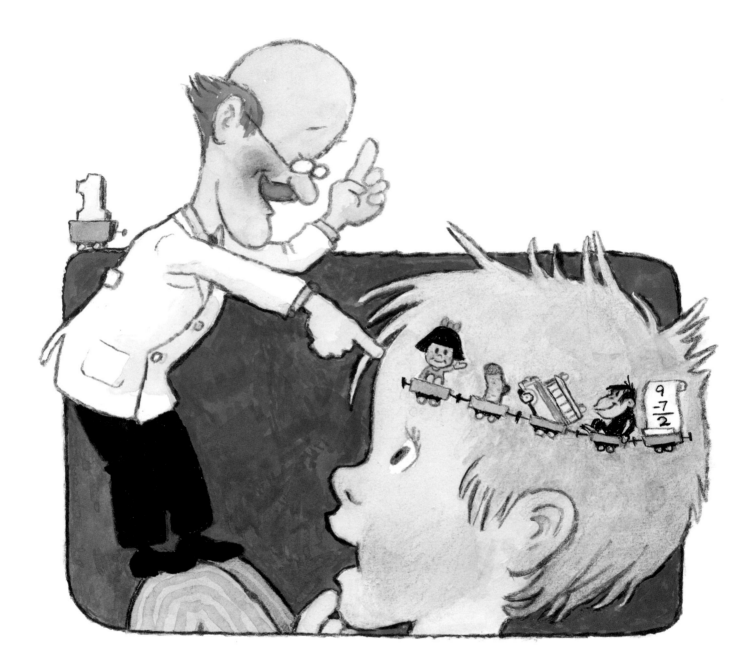

So load up your Brain Train and shout "ALL ABOARD!"
One car for each thing from today to be stored.

Remmy said to himself, "So much happened today...
The bug on the blackboard, the girl from Taipei.
The trip into town, the Museum of Art,
The math and the spelling, and how to be smart!"

Then Doctor Zeez had a bit more to add.
He took out his pen and his little white pad.

Here's a prescription to make you feel better.
Follow it closely — right to the letter!

He tore off the page and gave Remmy the note—
EARLY TO BED are the words that he wrote.

You need the whole nighttime — 9 hours, not less —
To make all the stops on the Brain Train Express.

The first place you'll stop is the Deep Sleep Hotel
Where your brain can relax 'til it's clear as a bell.
Your body is happy to stay there a while
To rest and to grow and to recharge your smile!

Then on to REM Station, to look left and right
At all the great scenes in the dreams of your night.

You might dream a wish that you hope will come true
An old thing that happened, or something brand new.

You'll unload your cars and make memory traces
And dream about birthdays or bullfrogs or braces.

The wombat and wildebeest might show up, too
And YOU'LL teach the kids how to add and spell "ZOO"!

FOUR TRIPS each night from Deep Sleep to REM Station—
A long way to go on your nighttime vacation!

When you wake up, you'll be rested and strong
And your good mood will shine like the sun all day long!

23

"Thank you," said Remmy to good Doctor Zeez.
"I've learned quite a lot from your sleep ABC's.
Now I must hop on my Brain Train and sleep.
I've got lots of good thoughts that I'd sure like to keep!"

COME TO THE STATION,
HOP ON THE TRAIN.
YOU DON'T NEED A TICKET —
JUST PACK UP YOUR BRAIN!
ROCK WITH THE RHYTHM
AND COUNT ALL THE SHEEP
CLICKETY-CLACK
TO THE LAND OF GOOD SLEEP!

When Remmy woke up the next morning he found
His trip on the train made the best brain around!

He could think, he could spell, and in math got an "A."
He hit a home run, and his pals yelled "HOORAY!"

So Remmy has figured out just what to do
And now Doctor Zeez wants to say this to YOU...

Tell me the things and the thoughts from your day
What did you do — did you work, did you play?
You must have a lot you can load on your train —
Things to remember and save in your brain!

But please don't forget, you can take me along.
I'll be the conductor, and sing you a song!
So pull up the covers and snuggle down deep —
Together we'll ride through the Land of Good Sleep.

COME TO THE STATION,
HOP ON THE TRAIN.
YOU DON'T NEED A TICKET —
JUST PACK UP YOUR BRAIN!
ROCK WITH THE RHYTHM
AND COUNT ALL THE SHEEP
CLICKETY-CLACK
TO THE LAND OF GOOD SLEEP!

Good Night.